Hello, Family Members,

Learning to read is one of the most important  early childhood. **Hello Reader!** books are desig[ned] become skilled readers who like to read. Begin[ners] read by remembering frequently used words like "the," "is," and "and"; by using phonics skills to decode new words; and by interpreting picture and text clues. These books provide both the stories children enjoy and the structure they need to read fluently and independently. Here are suggestions for helping your child *before*, *during*, and *after* reading:

Before
- Look at the cover and pictures and have your child predict what the story is about.
- Read the story to your child.
- Encourage your child to chime in with familiar words and phrases.
- Echo read with your child by reading a line first and having your child read it after you do.

During
- Have your child think about a word he or she does not recognize right away. Provide hints such as "Let's see if we know the sounds" and "Have we read other words like this one?"
- Encourage your child to use phonics skills to sound out new words.
- Provide the word for your child when more assistance is needed so that he or she does not struggle and the experience of reading with you is a positive one.
- Encourage your child to have fun by reading with a lot of expression...like an actor!

After
- Have your child keep lists of interesting and favorite words.
- Encourage your child to read the books over and over again. Have him or her read to brothers, sisters, grandparents, and even teddy bears. Repeated readings develop confidence in young readers.
- Talk about the stories. Ask and answer questions. Share ideas about the funniest and most interesting characters and events in the stories.

I do hope that you and your child enjoy this book.

— Francie Alexander
   Chief Education Officer,
   Scholastic's Learning Ventures

For Megan Wirtz, of Washington, D.C.
— K.M.

For Chico and Spike
— M.S.

ISBN 0-439-31943-9

Text copyright © 2002 by Kate McMullan.
Illustrations copyright © 2002 by Mavis Smith.
All rights reserved. Published by Scholastic Inc.
SCHOLASTIC, HELLO READER, CARTWHEEL BOOKS,
and associated logos are trademarks and/or
registered trademarks of Scholastic Inc.

Library of Congress Cataloging-in-Publication Data

McMullan, Kate.
    Fluffy goes to Washington / by Kate McMullan ; illustrated by Mavis Smith.
        p. cm. — (Hello reader! Level 3)
    Summary: When Fluffy goes on a trip with Maxwell's family, he gets to see some of the sights in the nation's capital.
    ISBN 0-439-31943-9
        [1. Guinea pigs—Fiction. 2. Washington (D.C.)—Fiction.] I. Smith, Mavis, ill. II. Title. III. Hello reader! Level 3.
PZ7.M47879 Flb 2002
[E]—dc21   2001049038

10 9 8 7 6 5 4 3 2 1   02 03 04 05 06

Printed in the U.S.A.   24
First printing, January 2002

FLUFFY

GOES TO WASHINGTON

by Kate McMullan
Illustrated by Mavis Smith

Hello Reader! — Level 3

SCHOLASTIC INC.

New York Toronto London Auckland Sydney
Mexico City New Delhi Hong Kong Buenos Aires

President Fluffy?

Fluffy went home with Maxwell
for Presidents' Day weekend.
Maxwell's family drove
to Washington, D.C.,
to visit Maxwell's cousin, Abby.
Fluffy went, too.

Maxwell's sister, Violet, sang
the whole way there:
"Fluffy-wuffy is a pig, E-I-E-I-O!"
It was a long trip.

When Maxwell's family got to
Washington,
Abby and her mom and dad
ran out to the car.
"Welcome!" they said.

"Hi, Maxwell!" said Abby.

"Hi, Violet! Hey, who is this?"

"This is Fluffy," said Maxwell.

Abby picked up Fluffy.

"Eleanor and Franklin will

love you!" she said.

Everybody loves me, thought

Fluffy.

Abby carried Fluffy to her room.

Maxwell carried his food.

Violet carried his treats.

"Fluffy, this is Franklin," said Abby.

She patted a brown gerbil.

"He is named after Franklin Roosevelt.
Roosevelt was president of the United
States more than 50 years ago."

"And this is Eleanor," said Abby.
She patted a honey-colored gerbil.
"She is named after the First Lady,
Eleanor Roosevelt."
Hi, guys, thought Fluffy.

Maxwell gave Fluffy food and water.
Violet gave him treats.
"You will stay here tomorrow
while we go see Washington,"
Maxwell told Fluffy.
No fair! thought Fluffy.
I want to see Washington, too!

The kids ran off to have pizza.
Eleanor and Franklin came
over to Fluffy's cage.
What president are you named after?
asked Eleanor.
Uh . . . said Fluffy.
President Fluffy? he said.

There was no President Fluffy,
said Franklin.
Too bad, said Fluffy.
He liked the sound of it.
President Fluffy!

**There was President
Washington,**
said Eleanor. **And
President Adams.**

And President Jefferson,
said Franklin.
And President Lincoln.

And President Teddy Roosevelt,
said Eleanor. **Don't forget him.**
Eleanor and Franklin went on and on.
They named president after president.

By morning, Fluffy had heard enough.
He climbed on top
of the wheel in his cage.

He jumped onto the desk.
Then he hurried over
to Maxwell's backpack
and ran inside.
Look out, Washington! he thought.
Here I come!

Hello, Mr. President

Later, Abby took Maxwell and Violet to the Mall. "Let's start with the National Air and Space Museum," she said.

They walked into a big building.

"Wow!" said Maxwell.

"There's the Kitty Hawk Flyer!"

Kitty hawk? thought Fluffy.

That sounded like a very scary
animal!

Fluffy peeked out of the backpack.

"Fluffy-wuffy!" said Violet.

Get me out of here, thought Fluffy.

"Fluffy!" said Maxwell. "How did you . . . "

Abby laughed. "I guess he wants
to see Washington, too," she said.

I've seen enough! thought Fluffy.

Maxwell held Fluffy up
to see the Kitty Hawk Flyer.
It was not a scary animal.
It was a machine with
two long wings.
"This is the very first airplane," said Abby.
Maxwell showed him Apollo 11.
"That took men to the moon!"
he said.
Cool, thought Fluffy.
Washington isn't so bad.

After a while, Abby said, "Let's go
to the Washington Monument."
They waited in a long line.
At last they got on an elevator.
Fluffy felt himself going up, up, up.
He got a funny feeling in his tummy.

At last they stepped out of the elevator.
"We are in the tallest building
in Washington," said Abby.
Maxwell held Fluffy up
to the window.
Fluffy looked out.
Aaaahhhhh! he thought.
Fluffy shut his eyes.
He did not open them again
until they were back on the ground.

"We have time to see the
Lincoln Memorial," said Abby.
I hope it is not tall, thought Fluffy.
They walked by the Reflecting Pool.
Ducks swam in it.
Hello, duckies! thought Fluffy.

"Here it is," said Abby.

Maxwell held Fluffy up.

"This is President Abraham Lincoln,"
he said.

Fluffy saw a statue of a big man
sitting in a big chair.

Hello, Mr. President, thought Fluffy.

"Abe Lincoln fought a war
to keep our country together,"
said Abby. "He was a great man."

Fluffy looked up at Mr. Lincoln.

So this is a president, he thought.

Fluffy thought he looked very kind.

But he looked worried, too.

Being president must be a hard job,

thought Fluffy.

When they got home, Maxwell
put Fluffy back into his cage.
Where have you been? said
Eleanor.
I've been to see the president,
said Fluffy. **President Abe Lincoln.**
Oh, right, said Franklin.
Fluffy snuggled down in his straw.
If I were named after a president,
he said, **I think I would like
to be called Abe.**

Fluffy at the White House

"Wake up, Fluffy!" said Violet.
"I am going to take you
to the White House! But *shhh!*
It is a secret."
**What's the big deal about
a white house?** thought Fluffy.

You won't get in, Franklin said
as Violet picked Fluffy up.
No, Eleanor said. **They will never
let a pig in the White House!**

Oh, yeah? thought Fluffy.
Well, you don't know this pig!

Violet, Abby, and Maxwell stood
in line for the White House Tour.
Violet kept Fluffy hidden
in her backpack.
He peeked out of a small opening.
But he could not see much.

A man on the lawn had a life-sized
cardboard cutout of the president.
A woman stood next to the cutout.
Snap! The man took her picture.
In the picture, it looked as if the
woman was standing with the president.

"Let's do that!" said Maxwell.

The kids ran over to the man with the camera.

Violet put down her backpack.

Fluffy peeked out.

He saw a white mouse.

Take the White Mouse White House Tour! the mouse said.

Why not? thought Fluffy.

Fluffy followed the mouse
through a mouse hole
into the White House.
They ran through a tunnel.
They stopped at a small hole.
**Take a peek at the White House
Library,** said the mouse.

Fluffy peeked. He saw a room
with many, many books.
They are all by American writers,
said the mouse.
So many books! thought Fluffy.

The mouse showed Fluffy the
Green Room.
And the Blue Room. And the Red Room.
For a white house, thought Fluffy,
it sure has lots of colors!

Now for the White House Pets!
said the mouse. He showed Fluffy
a picture of a dog named Fala.
And a dog named Millie.
Millie had puppies in the White House,
said the mouse.

The mouse showed Fluffy a picture
of a mockingbird and a raccoon
named Rebecca.

**The pets in the other picture
belonged to President Teddy
Roosevelt,** said the mouse.

Fluffy looked. His eyes grew big.

It was a picture of two guinea pigs.

All right! said Fluffy.

White House pigs!

After one more stop,
the White Mouse White House
Tour ended.
Fluffy popped out of a mouse hole.
At the same time, Maxwell,
Violet, and Abby came out of their
White House Tour.
"Fluffy!" said Maxwell. "How did you . . ."
I'll never tell, thought Fluffy.

Back at Abby's house,
Maxwell put Fluffy into his cage.
Eleanor and Franklin came over.
**You didn't get into the White House,
did you?** said Eleanor.
Yes, I did, said Fluffy.

Oh, right, said Franklin.

I can prove it, said Fluffy.

Oh, right, said Eleanor and
Franklin.

Tah-dah! said Fluffy.

Fluffy smiled.

A picture, he thought,

is worth a thousand words.